Discrimination Experienced
in the
Nursing Profession
by Minority Nurses

Discrimination Experienced
in the
Nursing Profession
by Minority Nurses

Fifty True Stories from Nurses
in New York City

Melvina Semper, DNP

iUniverse

DISCRIMINATION EXPERIENCED IN THE NURSING PROFESSION BY MINORITY NURSES FIFTY TRUE STORIES FROM NURSES IN NEW YORK CITY

iUniverse books may be ordered through booksellers or by contacting:

iUniverse
1663 Liberty Drive
Bloomington, IN 47403
www.iuniverse.com
1-800-Authors (1-800-288-4677)

ISBN: 978-1-4917-9751-8 (sc)
ISBN: 978-1-4917-9752-5 (e)

Library of Congress Control Number: 2016910745

Print information available on the last page.

iUniverse rev. date: 08/09/2016

To all the minority nurses who bravely shared their stories for the many years they have been abused, wrongfully terminated, experienced discrimination, passed over for promotion, underrepresented (and still are) in New York City hospitals, and also to the prospective nurses—to demonstrate to them that achieving your goals and dreams is within reach. When those who are ignorant put obstacles in your way, find that inner strength and remove those obstacles to continue on your path to great things. To those who shared their stories, kudos to you. Be strong, and never give up the fight. You are brilliant, smart, and educated. Finally, to my two children, Bilthorne and Flora, as well as my four grandchildren, who inspire me and ignite that spark within me to focus on social changes so they may live in a world of peace, equality, and justice for all.

Preface

This book contains fifty true stories of the experiences of minority nurses working in New York City hospitals. Its purpose is to create awareness and identify how racism and discrimination in the workplace affect minority nurses and the fabric of the nursing profession. This book reveals the ill treatment and lack of promotion, diversity, and moral support and other barriers minority nursing students and practicing nurses face on the job while working in New York City hospitals. Minority nurses are severely underrepresented within the health care setting in New York City in the twenty-first century. It highlights the need for strict laws, the enforcement of affirmative action, and the regulation of health care facilities to eradicate racism and discrimination minority nurses encounter in the workplace. Attention to these concerns is crucial at all local and state levels, as well as within New York State's Office of professional services.

Are you a minority nurse working in the community, nursing schools, or a hospital or nursing home setting in New York City? Have you experienced racism or discrimination on the job? Have you ever been passed over for promotion just because you are a minority nurse? Did you have the qualifications for a job and instead it was given to a white nurse less qualified? If you answered yes to any of these questions, then this book is for you to explore.

I was compelled to write this book to create awareness for all minority nurses in nursing schools and actively practicing as well as retired minority nurses. Throughout my nursing career as a registered nurse in New York City, I have experienced positive experiences, as well as negative ones. However, as I pursue my nursing career and have the opportunity to meet and work with many minority nurses, their struggles and the injustices they face in the workplace are becoming obvious. It is extremely difficult for me to turn a deaf ear to the many stories of the despicable treatment experienced by minority nurses. This book offers fifty true stories of the experiences of minority nurses in various health care settings throughout New York City. I have also received similar stories from nurses in other states, but New York City tops the list of complaints from minority nurses. It is my hope that minority nurses who are now venturing into the profession will be aware of these issues, obstacles, and challenges, as well as the disrespect and lack of promotion, within the nursing profession. I must warn you—some of these nurses' experiences may leave a bitter taste in your mouth and create a dislike for the nursing profession, but I do hope you learn about and address similar issues before they get out of control so you can stay focused on your love for the nursing profession. As you will see from these stories, diversity in the nursing profession is lacking, and this poses real threats to the health care system and the profession of nursing. I encourage all of you minority nurses, when faced with such problems, to tackle them head-on before they escalate and to find ways to de-escalate the issues you already face. Seek help, whether it is from your specific nurses association, your state board of nursing, a political figure or representative for your area or state, an attorney, or the news media, as you deem necessary. As you read these nurses' stories, you may realize that you have at some point in your career experienced the same or similar problems. Do not be fearful; instead find a support system or someone you can relate to, and stay on top of whatever the issue is until you reach some kind of resolution.

During my interviews with more than fifty nurses who worked at various hospitals in New York City, I discovered that many of the stories were either of the same nature or similar. I chose not to include multiple stories that showed such a similarity. The stories were just pouring in, many by word of mouth from those wanting to tell their stories. Finally, I decided to move forward with the fifty stories that appear in this book as they were presented to me by the many nurses I have interviewed.

—Melvina Semper, DNP

Story #

1

Only a White Nurse to Care for White Patients

Nurse Hernandez, RN, MSN, New York City

I completed nursing school and was excited to work as a registered nurse, which had been my dream. About three years ago, that dream of being a practicing nurse as well as my confidence in the nursing profession was shattered by my experience on the job as a minority nurse in a Brooklyn hospital setting.

It all began when a white female patient requested to have a white nurse care for her. My manager, who was inexperienced, only one year out of nursing school and working in her first managerial job, removed me from caring for the patient in question and replaced me with a white female nurse instead. The nurse manager left specific instructions going forward that this white patient would need to be assigned a white nurse.

I could not believe the openness of this racist act in the nursing profession. I am from a Hispanic background, but I had never experienced racism at this level. The charge nurse on my shift, who was an African American, informed me that this was a "common practice at this institution." She added that she was scared and worried about losing her job, so she felt she had no other alternative but to carry out such directives.

It turns out that this practice is widely considered to be acceptable, and it continues not just in this Brooklyn hospital but also in several other institutions where I have worked in the Bronx, Manhattan, and Westchester. Something is definitely wrong in our society when such a practice continues and is considered normal in the twenty-first century.

While driving to work one day, I heard on the radio a representative from a popular website, Monster.com, discussing the issue that more than three thousand nursing jobs per month are available and that it's a problem to fill those positions. One might ask, why? This is absolutely true, and this trend will continue until hospitals embrace a diversified workforce with equality for all across the board. This issue of racism can be easily rectified if the New York State Board of Nursing would place undercover representatives at institutions throughout the city to crack down on these practices. Until then, there will be a shortage of nurses who are willing to work within a hospital setting.

2

State, Local, and City Officials Fail to Protect Minority Nurses from Racism and Discriminations on the Job

S. Gonzalez, MSN, RN, Queens, New York City

After graduating nursing school, as a single mother of two young boys, ages six and nine, I was prepared, educated, and ready to pursue a nursing career where I could make a difference in people's lives. Oh, was I mistaken! I realized this after experiencing how minority nurses were treated like doormats. Discrimination in the hiring process and racism in the health care system are not only rampant but destructive to the fabric of the nursing profession. These practices continue to be a part of the tradition of minority nurses practicing in New York City. In the end, health care fails and the system and the nursing profession are adversely affected. The discrimination I have encountered in my five years as a practicing nurse stems from race, number one, followed by gender, ethnicity, age, and sexual orientation. The relevant associations, such as the American Nurses Association (ANA), have not done much to eradicate the practices of racism within health care institutions in which minority nurses work. Members' paying monetary dues seem to be of utmost importance to nursing organizations that supposedly are in place to represent nurses. To start solving these problems, the solution is very simple; the ANA and New York State Board of Nursing need to get on board and first mandate all hospitals to embrace a diversified workforce. Second, they need to disperse representatives to police these institutions, just as the state comes to institutions unannounced to see firsthand if procedures and guidelines are being implemented and carried out.

With these solutions, I will now delve into my experience as a minority nurse in New York City. First, let me reveal my background. I was born and raised in Puerto Rico but attended nursing school in New York City. After graduating, I started to work in a hospital in New York City on a medical surgical unit. After I had worked for four years on that unit, a manager's position became available. The requirements were at least two years' experience in my specialty area and a BSN in nursing. I had completed four and a half years and have a master's degree in nursing, which qualified me for the job. I applied for the job two days after it was posted on the jobs bulletin board. I was told by the human resources department that a night position was available instead. I told them that because of my present situation, a day position would be best for me at this time, and a day position was indeed posted. Three days later, I was informed the day position had been filled.

An informant who worked as a clerk in the human resources office told me in private that the practice of offering minority nurses night positions while offering the white nurses the day positions had been going on for years. When I queried human resources as to why this was happening, I was told that having the white nurses on the day shift made the hospital look good. I was not promoted because I was Hispanic. Two months later, I resigned and moved to another institution still within New York City where the same practice continued.

The question I would like to ask is: Should minority nurses continue in this profession, or should we find a means to beat these institutions at their own game by leaving them stranded to find nurses to do the work? Personally, I do believe the latter is the best option, or we should only work at institutions that truly embrace diversity and where justice prevails.

Story #

3

An Act of Homegrown Discrimination Conquered by Love

H. Irwin, MSN, RN, Brooklyn, New York

I am a Filipino nurse. I was born in the Philippines and attended nursing school in the United States. My nursing career began at a hospital in New York City, and after six years on the job, I moved to another hospital in Bronx, New York. The hospital I worked in, located in New York City, was approximately 85 percent white and 15 percent minority nurses. The way in which minority nurses were treated, spoken to, and given assignments was demeaning, spiteful, and, most importantly, widespread. I wanted to see if this kind of practice was in these two hospitals only. I was prompted to do some research to see if any other hospitals were doing this. My research uncovered a US Department of Health and Human Services (USDHS) survey, conducted in March 1996, which found that the nursing profession at this time was 90 percent white females. According to the USDHS, American society is evolving into an increasing lack of diversity and this lack of diversity in nursing is potentially harmful to the profession and the population it serves. Yet, twenty years later, the situation has gotten worse. The USDHS, as well as the American Nurses Association, has failed minority nurses miserably, and it is time for us all to protest, stop working in the United States, stop paying association fees, and take our cases to Albany for results. As long as we are nurses, we can work anywhere, local or abroad. In the end, the health care system as well as the health of innocent people will be jeopardized.

Today, I choose to run my own business and try to make a difference in the lives of those I care for. I remember how, in one day, I changed the mind of a white nurse manager whom I sat with after observing how poorly she treated minority nurses. I wanted to get firsthand knowledge as to why she had so much hatred for minority nurses burning inside of her. She said to me, "I do not like minorities, nor will I ever grow to like them." I think in a sense she was also yearning to speak with someone. As we sat and I questioned her, she broke down in tears and confided in me that as she was growing up, her father had taught her never to like or associate with minorities. After we sat talking for almost an hour, I convinced her we are human beings like herself and that her father did a poor job raising her. I told her he had misled and improperly educated her. There was a sigh of relief from her. I reiterated that minorities are human beings with the same ideas, needs, and aspirations. She cried in my arms and started apologizing over and over again. The same day, she went home and told her father, "Daddy, you were so wrong about minorities when I was growing up and are still wrong today. I am totally against your teachings and beliefs about minorities, and I discovered that at work today. Years of adhering to your teachings of hatred and discrimination have destroyed me emotionally, and going forward, I will be a changed person who will seek counseling to undo the years of damage you have inflicted upon me."

When I was about to write my story, I contacted this nurse manager, who is now retired, alerting her I would use our story. She agreed and also wanted me to apologize to others she had hurt in the past. Her words to me were: "I would like you to please apologize to any minority nurse I have hurt and caused severe grief. I am deeply sorry for my actions and the troubles I have caused as a nurse manager." I can clearly vow that I have helped eradicate one person's racism to where she was able to see and confront the demon in her and strive to make good. I showed her love, not hate.

Story #

Inhumane Treatment toward Minority Nurses

D. Lowinsky, BSN, RN, Staten Island, New York

I was born in Russia. My decision to practice nursing in the United States was, in my opinion, a mistake. I took some time off from working in a hospital in New York City after three years on the job. The racism, disrespect, and bullying of minority nurses forced me to leave the hospital setting. Either I stayed and did something I would regret, or I stayed on duty and tolerated the inhumane treatment that was being handed down to minority nurses. I returned to the hospital setting after two years away from the concentration camp I had previously been working in. This time, I opted to work in a hospital in Brooklyn. Was I in for a shock! I had been hoping that things perhaps had gotten better, but instead, they had gotten worse. My first observation was that minority nurses were offered positions on the night shifts. After I got settled in and started to query why minorities were working the night shift and not the day shift, the response I received was that the vice president of nursing had told one of her white managers, "I am looking for slim white girls with short skirts to work the day shift." This statement came directly from a white nurse manager who confided in me. I was speechless when I heard this statement. This then answered my lingering question as to why minority nurses were not working on the day shift.

Being a Russian nurse and 190 pounds, I knew this was a work environment I did not want to be in. There were several other Russian nurses who encouraged me to stay because we also had to take care of our families back home. Again, I stayed on the job for three years, got some finances together, and opened my own business unrelated to nursing. It was a loss to the nursing profession but a victory for me. My advice to minority nurses is to fight as a group and not individually; there is power in numbers, so please, if nursing is your passion, do not be forced out of it. We should work as a team because teamwork divides the task and doubles our success, and together everyone can achieve a successful outcome. I discourage young minorities from going into this profession for fear of going through the same experience and will continue to do so.

One experience I had was as follows. One night, as the only Russian nurse on duty, I was instructed by a white nurse manager who had just two years on the job to go into a patient's room and clean up a water spill on the floor. This was not even a room I was assigned. This infuriated me so much that I actually just looked at her and shook my head in disgust. Facing discrimination in the workplace for minority nurses is like venturing out into Nursing 101, the very first course in the nursing profession. Nursing 101 for minority nurses includes fighting racism and discrimination on the job.

For me, this was my introduction to the world of professional nursing. I discussed this experience with a colleague who worked at another institution in Long Island City. She informed me she had experienced similar issues in the hospital she presently worked at. I indicated to my colleague that the nursing profession was one with a shortage and a great need. Finding a job where her service was accepted and appreciated was more important than any amount of money. Two months later, my friend and colleague quit her job and went back to Russia, where she is happily practicing as a nurse.

Story #
5

Racism and Discrimination Contribute to the Nursing Shortage

T. Nidhi, FNP, Long Island, New York

As New York City struggles to find solutions to the nursing shortage, minority nurses are removing themselves from the profession, especially within the hospital settings. Nursing schools also are not proactive in recruiting or attracting minority nursing students because many of the schools are working with hospitals. They begin implementing discrimination in the schools, which ultimately filters into the health care settings. The nursing school I attended had only a handful of minority nursing students and very few minority nursing faculty. In most cases, the minority faculty get a position only if the school is unable to find white faculty.

I was born in India and attended nursing school in New York City.

One day, I explained to my father what I had observed in terms of the discrimination. My father immediately removed me from the school and said, "My money will not be spent in schools like this to foster racism and discrimination." He placed me in another school with about 70 percent minority and 30 percent

12

white students. The atmosphere was much better. The faculty was about 40 percent minorities and 60 percent white—a better ratio to deal with. Discrimination still did exist among faculty and students; it was just that it was not as obvious as in the previous school I had attended. After graduation, I also looked for a hospital where there was some diversity in the workplace. A dynamic, diversified workforce is unstoppable and leads to insurmountable success. I learned from those early experiences, so once I got into institutions that promoted this practice, I was aware, educated, and equipped to take on any challenge of racism or discrimination. During my working experiences as a practicing nurse, I have seen acts of discrimination and decided to send anonymous letters to the New York State Nursing Association with the persons involved and the name of the hospital.

The New York State Nursing Association has not made any effort to investigate my findings. I did not reveal my identity because I was still working at the institution. I have no way of verifying if any actions have been taken since I left that institution, but I know for sure these practices still continue. I have since moved into a different area of nursing practice where I have more autonomy and respect from the people I work with. I presently work as a nurse practitioner in an all Indian urgent-care facility.

Hospitals throughout New York City is presently facing severe inadequate staffing of nurses which has impacted patient care and patient care outcomes. Hospitals are seeing drastic decrease in patient's census due to lack of nursing staff mix to provide competent patient care. The lack of nurses to work puts added stress on other nurses, which eventually results in fast turnover and increased cost to institutions.

Quality health care should be a top priority in New York City hospitals, but without a more diversified workplace the possibilities of quality care is bleak. With increased available nursing positions at home and abroad, experienced minority nurses have more options than ever before, thus leaving hospitals with an increased workforce instability.

Story #

6

A Minority Nurse's Simple Solutions to Eradicate Racism and Discrimination

L. Lafonte, BSN, RN, Bronx, New York

As a practicing nurse in New York City, I believe in providing solutions to problems; therefore, my story will take on a different format. To fix the issues of racism, discrimination, nonpromotion, and inequality in the workplace that minority nurses face today, institutions should be mandated by law to:

1. Mentor and adequately orient new minority nurses on the job for the positions they are hired for—mentoring is the key to retention and work satisfaction. When great minds work together, great things flourish.
2. Impose hefty fines on institutions for practices of racism and discrimination.
3. Implement an investigative body that will check and verify the qualifications for managerial positions within these institutions.
4. Institute policies for diversity statewide in all institutions and close down those facilities that fail to do so.

5. Investigate minority claims of being qualified, and in many cases more qualified, for managerial positions than the white nurses who are placed in them.
6. Investigate salaries of minority nurses and compare them with those of white nurses—Are the salaries the same? Do their salaries differ, and if so, why?
7. Investigate under what circumstances minority nurses are fired from their jobs—I have witnessed cases firsthand where white nurses were given one, two, three, or four verbal warnings and minority nurses were fired without even a verbal warning.

In my sixteen years of nursing practice, I have experienced all the injustices listed here in various hospitals I have worked in as a Haitian American nurse. I have seen other cases on the job that demonstrated a discrepancy in the treatment of minority and white nurses. There was one case in which twelve white nurses were only suspended for taking narcotics for their personal use and six minority nurses with the same offenses were fired. When I complained to the vice president (VP) of nursing, who was white, her response was, "If you want to keep your job, then leave things alone. You see nothing, and you say nothing." I went home that day and could not believe a VP of nursing was part of this practice. My husband strongly encouraged me to leave the job, and I did.

After careful consideration, I decided to address the problem from where it could possibly stem from. I thought that was nursing schools. I became a nursing faculty member. This role has similar issues, but with more autonomy, I can start making small changes. One of my first observations in nursing schools was how severely underrepresented minority students were and how few minority nursing faculty there were to teach, train, and educate future nurses. In my role as a nursing faculty member, I decided to use this platform to make some changes. Diversity, love, justice, and equality are open discussions in my classrooms.

Story #

7

Lack of Diversity and Increased Prejudice on the Job for Minority Nurses

J. Catalina BSN, RN, Brooklyn, NY

I am a registered nurse who has worked in various hospitals throughout New York City. I am from the Philippines and migrated to the United States twenty-one years ago. I have worked at two hospitals in the Bronx, three hospitals in Brooklyn, and two in New York City. During my years of working at these institutions, I found that racism and discrimination toward minority nurses existed in all of them, though some were more pronounced than others. Especially in New York City, many hospitals lack diversity, and if you do find minority nurses on duty, they are often placed on the night shifts. I have seen frequent and ongoing degrading treatment of minority nurses, from getting unfair assignments to being denied holidays when they were warranted and being passed over for promotion, despite having the required qualifications. I have worked within hospitals where there are so-called VIP floors. Minority nurses will not be assigned to these floors even when they require floating and it's their turn to float. As previously noted, all the hospitals I have worked in in New York City have a big problem with racism in the nursing departments. At times, minority nurses are assigned heavy patients, and when they requested help, their white coworkers would refuse. Complaining to the white managers was a waste of time. They look at you as if you are a troublemaker. Racism, discrimination, and prejudice are alive and well in the nursing profession.

One of the main reasons for minority nurses removing themselves from hospital settings is institutional racism. Minorities are constantly passed over for promotions even when they have proven themselves on the job and have the qualifications. All minority nurses need to make a conscious effort to address discrimination when noted in the workplace. Whether it occurs in nursing schools or the workplace, we all need to advocate for each other to institute change in the nursing profession. My hope and my prayer for all minority nurses is that they join forces and eradicate racism from within the institutions that encourage it.

8

Widespread Racism in Nursing Schools and on Minority Nurses in the Workplace

P. Anderson, MSN, RN, Queens, New York City

Battling racism and discrimination as a practicing nurse in New York City was and still is a deeply rooted issue for me. Various facilities and different regions have different situations, and my experiences with racism were more widespread in some places than in others.

I am an African American nurse who was born and raised in New York City. My parents often saw and experienced racism and discrimination when I was growing up. Today I begin to wonder if their fight was in vain. At thirty years old, I find that racism is just as rampant today as it was during my parents' years.

The first bout of racism I experienced occurred when I was in nursing school. It appeared that in the eyes of faculty members, giving minority students an A was like committing a crime. One day, out of frustration and disgust, I challenged this practice. I was in a class of twenty-five students, and we were all given an assignment to write a paper. In the class were eight minority students, and the remaining seventeen students were white. The assignment was not difficult; when the grades were assigned by a white instructor, all the white students received an A. However, for the minority students, the highest grade was a B–, a clear indication of discrimination in the classroom.

There were no indications on my paper to show where I could improve going forward, so I decided to meet with the instructor to discuss my grade. His response was, "Your paper was very good."

I then replied, "Where is the reflection in my grade that my paper was very good?"

The instructor was speechless and at a loss for words.

I said, "Could I redo my paper to get a better grade?"

He responded, "Sure."

I had a plan I knew would prove that discrimination existed in this particular nursing school. I was a friend of a white student who had received an A, so I asked her if I could keep her paper for a day just to see where I went wrong. On her paper, there were many spelling errors as well as grammatical mistakes. However, I copied her paper, not changing any of the words or the format, put my name on it, and submitted it to the instructor a few days later. He gave me a B+.

It was time for a shake-up in this school. I then said to the professor, "We have a problem here. The paper I submitted was my friend's paper, and here is mine."

He was again speechless. I informed him of what I had done and told him that if my grade was not changed, this would go viral and the news media, the dean, and the entire school would be informed of his grading tactics. He immediately changed my grade to an A. From that day forward, I went on to colleges with my eyes wide open, armed and ready should this ever be repeated again. My continuous fight throughout my college years was necessary because this grading system for minority students was widespread throughout the college. My goal was to prevent this practice from occurring as long as I was attending that college.

Minority Nurses Frequently Passed Over for Promotion despite Being Adequately Qualified

D. Lewis, RN, MSN, Brooklyn, New York

As a minority nurse working in New York City, I have experienced racism and discrimination and been passed over for promotion. Like many other nurses, I am compelled to tell my story so other minority nurses will be aware and as a result will stay focused and help to weed out this practice encountered in several, if not all, New York City hospitals. Racism in America exists and continues to thrive. There have been minimal changes in eradicating racism in the United States, but we still have far to go. Being a practicing minority nurse in New York is not much different from the recent shootings, brutality, and deaths of minorities by mostly white police officers across the city and statewide. We ask ourselves, "Where is the justice?" Complaints have been made against several hospitals that have been involved in discriminatory and racist practices, yet nothing has been done to address them. I have also made several complaints to city officials and, of course, they were swept under the rug.

There needs to be daily investigations of these institutions, and those found to be involved should be held accountable. Better yet, these institutions should be shut down or fined, and there should be some form of imprisonment to send a clear message that these practices will not be tolerated in New York City. As a minority nurse practicing in New York City, I have seen it all when it comes to the demeaning and racist unfairness on the job experienced by minority nurses.

When I was asked to tell my story, I was thrilled to know that someone was willing to take this step so many minority nurses' voices can be heard. Those within these institutions who encourage these practices need to take a hard look at how they are destroying the nursing profession and take the issue of racism home because it is homegrown and needs to be first addressed there.

Communities need to come together to help address this poison that is so widespread in New York City. Until then, we will all have a constant battle that we must fight day in and day out to work in peace in New York City in a profession we all love. Let it be known that minorities are as much a part of the fiber of this country as anyone else.

Story #
10

A Minority Nurse Took Her Discrimination Case to Court

V. Washington, MSN, NP, Staten Island, New York

Laws and regulations against blatant discrimination are in place in New York City, but the sad truth is that it does not stop racism or discrimination in the workplace against minority nurses. Too often in institutions where I have worked, some white patients will request to have white nurses care for them, and this request will be granted by nurse managers who in many instances are white. A group of Filipino nurses in California filed a class action lawsuit. When they won their case of discrimination on the job, it was a wake-up call for some institutions, which later temporarily started to create diversity in the workplace, though their efforts did not last for a long time. I have also in the past filed a lawsuit for discrimination on the job and won. In my case, this particular employee knew it was a solid case; the institution also realized this and settled out of court. From a minority nurse to other minority nurses, if you experience any discrimination on the job, you should move ahead individually or as a group and file lawsuits against institutions involved in this practice. These lawsuits may take some time, but setting an example with one, two, or three institutions is worth the time. Do not believe for one moment you do not have options. Do not accept or tolerate these practices, because if you do, it will only get worse.

My experience of discrimination in the workplace was being passed over for promotion. A head nurse position was advertised. Applicants needed a bachelor's degree, and I had a master's degree. This position was offered to a white nurse with an associate degree who was in school pursuing a bachelor's degree. It was for this incident I filed a lawsuit and won. Prior to my lawsuit, I made several complaints to the human resources department and nursing administration, who appeared defensive and unreceptive to my complaints.

My advice to all minority nurses is to arm yourself, keep a paper trail, and record the names of witnesses and persons involved in your problems on the job just in case you need to file a case at a later date so that presenting your case will be a smooth process. Let's all get on the bandwagon and continue our efforts to weed out racism and discrimination in the workplace. The race is on. Let's run it together to maintain the true integrity of the nursing profession.

Story #

11

Underrepresentation for Minority Nurses

S. Braithwaite, RN, BSN, Long Island, New York

In New York City, registered nurses represent a large number of health care workers. Minority representation in the nursing profession is stagnant. I come from a Caribbean background, and hard work is integrated into my aspiration to be successful; therefore, pursuing my education with obstacles by the wayside was very easy. I had learned how to remove obstacles.

Telling my story of how racism and discrimination is infiltrating the health care system may not only help in creating awareness but perhaps provide information as to how it contributed to the nursing shortage and nurses not wishing to work in hospitals. The inequality, barriers, and struggles of minority nurses are as real today as they were during slavery. It is my hope that nursing educators will utilize their expertise to implement strategies that will have a positive impact on minority nursing students as well as practicing nurses. Nursing school has a platform in place to start addressing racism and discrimination on the job. During my years in nursing school, racism and discrimination did exist. A white instructor once said to me, "You will never make it in nursing school. Your future is in my hands, and I can make it really difficult for you." This all happened only because I challenged my grade.

Today, I am happy to say I have completed nursing school, received my PhD, and am a nursing faculty member who will make a difference using my platform. I also own my own business, and I hire nurses. So to all minority nurses out there who were told at some point you could not make it, take my experience and your will to succeed to rise to great heights.

Nursing has a revolving door. We never know whom we will run into within the nursing profession. Let's all be respectful of each other and encourage, motivate, and inspire one another. When others utilize discrimination or ignorance to impede your success, greet them always with love and respect. When your white nurse managers approach you with racist comments, respond with equality and justice for all. The only time we will see changes in the nursing profession is when you decide to take the first step toward real change.

Story #

12

A Nursing Student's Exposure to Racism

M. Rodriquez, MSN, RN, Bronx, New York

I am not a practicing nurse, but a BSN nursing student in my final year of nursing school. I am telling my story to make other minority students aware of what I went through in nursing school. I am a Hispanic American who was trained and educated in the nursing profession in New York City. During my years in nursing school, I became friends with African Americans and Indians, as well as students from Russia, Africa, the Caribbean, and other minority students who are from various other countries.

My story is as true as theirs. I hear their stories every day and have witnessed their struggles in nursing school. The learning environment for minority students was full of tension; it was rigid, nonsupportive, and unfair. We always worked twice as hard to prove ourselves and to fit in. Minority students were all viewed negatively, referred to as incompetent, and treated poorly because of their background, culture, race, or the color of their skin and for being minorities. Minority students were too intimidated to address the issue of racism for fear of retaliation and failing their classes. Minority students were always targeted; some minority students described it as the "weeding-out process." I personally was told by a white instructor that some students would be weeded out before the end of the semester.

Instructors grilled targeted students on weaknesses and made fun of them instead of implementing strategies to help them to succeed. Before the end of the term, several minority students who were targeted would be out of the program, not because they failed the class but because they challenged the instructor or questioned their grades.

This practice is evident when minorities are given completely different exams from the white students. After our exams, we would all meet and discuss our exams. Several white students would be puzzled as to what we were discussing because according to them they had received a different exam, which, in their own words, was "much easier." I refused to buckle up and be defeated; I pursued, persevered, and removed obstacles along the way just to complete my dream of being a nurse. Minority students were fully aware that the nursing program at this New York City nursing school was intentionally made very difficult for minorities so they would not succeed.

Several instructors would tell us not to study certain content for exams, and on the day of the exam, 90 percent of the information we were told not to study would be on the exams. This was done in an effort to fail us. The Caribbean nurses I observed seemed to have less difficulty because many of them said they had read the entire book if they had to and they totally disregarded information from instructors to study only for the exam. This technique of studying did give them an edge over other minority students who were born and raised in the United States. As several Caribbean students noted, "We never have multiple-choice questions; we have to know our stuff to pass exams in which we have to write summaries instead of the guessing games here in the US." We have the same issues and discrimination against us, but we still try, study hard, and avoid challenging our grades even though in many instances we have reasons to. Trying to be on our best behavior is what helps us to pass our classes.

I strongly recommend that all nursing students do their research and choose nursing schools wisely before moving ahead and spending their hard-earned money in schools that will set them up for failure.

Story #

13

A Workforce without Diversity Is Destructive to the Nursing Profession

M. Jones, RN, BSN, Queens, New York

Lack of diversity in the workplace is enough evidence for state officials to intervene and take action to dismantle the racism and discrimination within the nursing profession in New York City. Nursing schools should be mandated to reflect diversity in the workplace because it is not only the lack of diversity that sends the message that racism exists; the practice in nursing schools is another root cause that fans the flame of promoting racism, which is later integrated into practice. I can recall in nursing school in our skills labs we had all white manikins; none were reflective of minorities—another seed planted for racism in the nursing profession.

Looking back years later, I can see clearly that racism stemmed from nursing schools like the one I attended. Just like all the manikins for us to practice our nursing skills on, all my nursing instructors were white. If we want to see real changes in the nursing profession, we all need to focus on nursing schools and what goes on in nursing programs. We need to start diversifying nursing faculties, along with the classrooms and nursing skills

31

labs where the root of this toxin of racism is taught, practiced, and encouraged.

We were trained in nursing school to care for patients, but which type of patients? Today within many health care settings in New York City, the treatment of minority nurses is far from equal to that of their white counterparts. Minority nurses are held to a different standard than white nurses. How do I know? I have lived it, witnessed it, and worked in the environment that embraces this practice. We are trained to care for the sick and provide them with the best quality of care. We were not trained to fight racism and discrimination in the workplace. Please remember, a disease in one place is a disease everywhere; therefore, it is imperative that this disease be treated urgently. If we are to accomplish great strides in fighting racism, we must not only act or plan; we must believe it can be done.

Story #

14

A Nurse's Constant Fight against Racism

S. Henderson, BSN, RN, Long Island, New York

Who would believe in the twenty-first century minority nurses are constantly faced with racism and discrimination in the nursing profession in New York City? Nursing is a profession that should be based on caring for the less fortunate, sick people. Instead, minority nurses spend most of their working profession fighting ongoing discrimination, racism, harassment, disrespect, lack of promotion, inequality, and educational and promotional obstacles on the job. I was a pregnant minority nurse on the job in a Long Island hospital, my first job out of nursing school. It left me with a feeling of pure disgust, a bad taste in my mouth, because of the injustice I experienced and witnessed on the job.

After working six months on the job, I approached my nurse manager, who was white, and asked if I could get my evaluation. It is standard practice for all institutions to give you one shortly after orientation. Out of nowhere, the manager's response was, "Just to inform you, there are no special privileges for pregnant nurses around here." I was very surprised by her comment because at no time had I requested any special accommodations while on the job.

I had never received an evaluation of my performance to that point except the comment made by the nurse manager. The next day, I was contacted by a nurse advocate, telling me she had heard of the treatment I had received from this manager. She wanted to know if she could assist and meet with the manager. I told her no, since this was my first encounter. Big mistake! What I experienced on the job going forward I would not wish on any new graduate or experienced nurse. Two days later, the manager approached me and said, "I would like you to sign a learning contract." When I asked about the reason, she indicated it was a contract for reorientation. I was confused because I had never once been told in the six months I was on the job that my work was not up to standards. I refused to sign this so-called learning contract and asked a few nurses on the job, who were mostly white, if they had had to sign a learning contract. They all said no and that they had never heard of a learning contract. One white nurse pulled me to the side and said, "Be careful with that manager. She is not a nice person. She has spent years mistreating minority nurses, and nothing seems to be done."

I reported to work two days later, and while I was giving the report at the end of my shift, my manager called me and said, "You need to go into that patient's room and pick up the garbage on the floor."

As a new nurse just out of school, I did not want to cause any problems so after giving the report, I went to clean up the garbage. The next day, my manager came to me and instructed me to do the same thing. None of the rooms she instructed me to clean up belonged to me, and the patients were not patients I had cared for. I noticed things seemed to be getting out of hand so I immediately went to human resources after work to file a complaint. I waited for some resolution for a week, but nothing was done by human resources, so I proceeded to write a letter to the CEO of the hospital, who to this day has never responded. This was a nonunion hospital, so minority nurses had no form of support. I heard from a staff member the manager was informed by human resources of my complaint. I was now targeted, harassed, and threatened with being placed back on orientation. I was called into the manager's office and told that my life would be nothing but pure misery while working there. I decided then I would not go into her office again alone. When I returned to work two days later, I worked the night shift from 7:00 p.m. to 7:00 a.m. I was six months pregnant when a note was left on the unit for other nurses to see that I would resume four more days with a preceptor who was not informed she had to precept me. Everyone was very puzzled as to why I was now going back on orientation.

The preceptor, a white nurse with two years on the job, spent all night at the nursing station, not observing what I was doing or initiating any strategies for me to improve my performance on the job. When I asked for assistance to help turn patients, none was provided. I tried to do the best I could to help my assigned patients. Several nurses on the unit questioned why I was placed back on orientation. I had no answer for them because I also did not know why I was placed back on orientation, except out of pure hatred from this nurse manager. I was told that this was common practice toward minority nurses, and each year, it got worse. This particular nurse manager had a history of firing minority nurses in the blink of an eye, and nothing had been done about this problem. The harassment on the job became so severe that I would not want to go to work but forced myself to. I hired an attorney, who I do believe worked for the hospital instead. In the area where I lived, a white attorney was all I could get, so I did so out of desperation. Looking back, I see I should have searched for a minority attorney.

I made a complaint to the Equal Employment Opportunity Commission (EEOC), which in my opinion was also a waste of my time. There was no positive outcome, and my case was not properly investigated. I was contacted weeks later by human resources when they found out I had filed a complaint with the EEOC. The human resources department and the facility's attorney wanted me to withdraw the case from the EEOC. I refused to do that and was suspended two days later without any verbal warning in the past or as of that time.

At various institutions, if there is an issue with an employee, disciplinary measures move in stages; for example, first one would receive a verbal warning. I received none. Instead, I was suspended and later terminated. Even while I was on termination, human resources called and told me if I removed my complaint from the EEOC, my job would be reinstated. I explained all this to the EEOC, and again nothing was done to address the problem. I refused to do what they were asking and remained terminated. The best advice I received was from a nurse advocate who encouraged me to stop paying attorney fees to an ineffective attorney and move on to find another job. The nurse advocate's words were: "Find a job, and then sit back and wait for what will become of your manager." So she said and so it was done. Nine months later, my manager was investigated for racism and discrimination in the workplace and was escorted from the hospital by security guards after investigations turned up that she was corrupt.

This was a bittersweet moment. My belief in God is strong, and I always tell myself when people try to do bad to me, I will turn them over to God and then wait for him to take action. This justice system works for me and continues to work. I have no desire to work within hospital settings; however, with encouragement from a nursing advocate, I later ventured out and found another job I am pleased with. But I am aware of what goes on with minority nurses and I am better prepared to handle any such situation should it occur again. In New York City, we have a nurses association, a state board of nursing, the EEOC, and state officials to help with these issues, but the only person I can thank for helping me through this dark time in my life as a new grad is the nurse advocate. May God bless her!

The Effects of Racism in the Nursing Profession

D. Bassenet, FNP, Brooklyn, New York

A prominent and particularly negative form of prejudice in America is racism. This is manifested in the attitudes of several white nurse leaders toward minority nurses. It poses an adverse impact on the health care working environment, the nursing profession, and recipients of the health care rendered. Selective mistreatment of minority nurses simply undermines the work and experiences of hardworking professional nurses.

During my nursing career, seven years to be exact, I, like other minority nurses, have seen the mistreatment minority nurses receive on the job from their white counterparts. Immediate action is needed to halt this trend of discrimination and racism throughout New York City hospitals. I have seen minority nurses train white nurses with associate degrees on the job, who shortly after, in some instances, are promoted into positions that require a bachelor's degree. Equality and justice in the profession of nursing does not exist for minorities.

The American Nurses Association (ANA) and state boards of nursing have an obligation to all nurses in every state to get involved and implement strategies to address and eradicate racism in hospitals statewide. Policies are not difficult to construct, and they are needed to promote strict guidelines for diversity and address racism in the nursing profession. Just as we have patient safety goals and standards of practice for all institutions, we also need to do the same with regard to racism and discrimination in these same institutions. The nursing curriculum from the undergraduate to graduate level is in need of changes. The recruitment of culturally diversified nursing school faculty, as well as diversity within the health care settings in New York City, needs to be mandated to follow strict guidelines of removing racism and discrimination in the workplace.

Story #

16

A Nurse's Story to Create Awareness of Racism and Discrimination

Y. Sanders, FNP, New York City

Bravo to all minority nurses in New York City who have gone above and beyond to stand up to racism and discrimination in the nursing profession. I am glad so many have chosen to share their stories to educate and create awareness and be a support system to potential nurses, practicing minority nurses, and those who are now retired and have had similar experiences. There may be other minority nurses who at this very moment are experiencing what I and many others have experienced in the nursing profession.

The racial tension in the workplace at times is so high that many minority nurses just pray for their shifts to come to an end. I have a friend who is an exceptional nurse from Portugal. She endured a mental breakdown on the job and was sent to the hospital's emergency room. To this day, she has not returned to work, having been permanently damaged psychologically by the treatment she received from white managers on the job.

I strongly believe that just as police officers in New York City are given terrorism training, both nurses and police officers should receive racism training and ongoing yearly training should be made mandatory and required as part of their job requirements. If our government is spending huge sums of money to fight terrorists, the same should be done to fight racism. After all, hatred and racism are breeding grounds for terrorist activities.

As a practicing nurse in New York City, I have seen the hatred, racism, and discrimination that all minority nurses face. I was born in the United States and attended nursing school in New York City. It was troubling in that the same racism I experienced in nursing school is even worse on the job. Everyone from VP of nursing, administrators, and nursing faculty was white. Honestly, I am more scared of racism in New York City than any form of terrorism.

There are qualified minority nurses in New York who can fill many of these same jobs, but they are never given a chance because of the heightened racism and discrimination within the nursing profession. These practices still exist in the workplace, and minorities who speak up or attempt to expose them are often fired, targeted as troublemakers, passed up for promotion, and given challenging nursing assignments as a way to force them out of the institution.

Some minorities take the bait, do just that, and are prematurely forced out of their jobs. However, you do have some minorities who stand up and fight. I encourage all minorities to undertake the same fight for justice in the workplace. Politicians speak about building walls for illegal immigrants. We need walls built to control racism, in that those responsible are held accountable and placed behind bars (imprisonment), taking care of business at home before moving out into someone else's territory needs to be a priority of fighting racism in New York City.

Story #
17

The Power of a Nurse Advocate

J. Bernard, FNP, Staten Island, New York

I am a nurse advocate who sometimes represents nurses on the job when there needs to be some resolution and meeting of the minds. Today, I still practice as a nurse and intervene when I observe any blatant form of racism or discrimination on the job. I decided to tell my story because, while advocating recently for a minority nurse in New York City, I was appalled by what minority nurses deal with on a daily basis. I was called by a nurse who lives and works in Long Island, New York, to sit in on a meeting that was scheduled with her nurse educator about her performance. This nurse had complained to human resources and the EEOC regarding the treatment she was receiving on the job. Some of what this nurse revealed to me that took place in a hospital on Long Island was shocking, and I could not believe it. Therefore, I decided to attend the meeting with her. She was told this meeting would be with the nurse educator alone.

While waiting for the educator to join us in the scheduled meeting, I observed five white women approaching—the vice president of nursing, the nurse educator, and three nurse managers within the hospital. They did not expect to see this inexperienced minority nurse with a representative. I introduced myself and showed my New York state identification since I was a practicing nurse working within a state job. Suddenly the meeting was cancelled, and all five white nurses scattered and took a detour. When I asked why the meeting was cancelled, I received the response, "We were not prepared for this. The nurse did not inform us she was bringing someone." My response was "Just as she was informed she was meeting with one person but instead there are five of you for the meeting. The same applies to all five of you, who never informed the nurse that several others would be in the meeting." I could only imagine how they would have railroaded that nurse in a meeting with five white nurse administrators against one newly graduated minority nurse. They did not know this minority nurse was ahead of the game and had an experienced minority nurse present to turn to for help. This was an obvious blow to their plan.

My presence, years of experience, and New York state identification instilled some fear in them, and as a result, the meeting to continue the harassment of this nurse was suddenly cancelled. I could positively say without a doubt that racism in this Long Island hospital exists and is on the rise. This I observed when I personally interviewed several minority nurses at this particular institution. Shame! Shame! Shame on you!

Story #
18

How White Nurse Managers Plot to Mistreat Minority Nurses

L. Delevia, MSN, RN, Bronx, New York

As a Filipino nurse in New York City, having white nurse managers was disastrous to my nursing career and those of many others after me. On several occasions, I was instructed by my nurse manager to give minority nurses assignments where patients were extremely aggressive, agitated, and combative or were placed on suicide watch. Deep down, I knew it was wrong so one day after taking a step back and reevaluating what I was doing, I confronted my manager and told her I would not be part of this plot. Her response was, "I am sure you want to keep your job." I went home and told my husband what had happened. I also filed a complaint with the human resources department, who did nothing. With the support of my husband and his encouragement, I left the job two months later. I resigned and sought another job elsewhere to prevent getting fired and further ruining my career. This manager in question remains at this institution and continues with the discrimination within the workplace, utilizing minority nurses to do her dirty work. Many minority nurses, some of whom are foreigners, will go along with the plot just to keep their jobs and be able to take care of their families here and abroad. A colleague called me a month after I left the job, saying, "I think I know why you left the job." She explained to me she had been asked to do the same thing I was doing and this was completely against her beliefs and values as a nurse. She wanted to know what she should do at this point. I encouraged her to start looking for another job because if she stayed on board she would either be harassed or ultimately fired. I also informed her that going to the human resources department was not worth the effort because nothing would get done. She took my advice and within a month left the job.

It is essential that facilities such as these have standard policies across the board for hospitals to abide by, and if they do not adhere to the policies, they should be held responsible for their actions. These problems can be fixed. They are not rocket science. Call your state and local officials, as well as the New York State Board of Nursing, send letters, and demand changes in these health institutions. After all, our tax dollars are paying their salaries.

Messages of Racism Sent to Patients

J. Travet, RN, MSN, Long Island, New York

I worked in a hospital in Long Island, New York, where the entire hierarchy was white, from the CEO to the clinical ancillary service staff. A panel of fourteen hospital representatives had no minority members on board; this speaks for itself. Perhaps minorities should not work at these institutions. I must say this; no matter how much racism and discrimination exist in the workplace, one thing I know for sure is they cannot function without minority nurses. Minority nurses, including myself, are visionary leaders who are capable of creating solutions to problems and creating healthy, diversified working environments.

Hospitals like these send the wrong message to employees and patients alike. While I was working in this particular institution, it was very obvious that racism and discrimination were integrated into every department within this institution. The New York State Nursing Association's elected officials should be held accountable for not investigating these serious issues that minority nurses encounter in the workplace. Many of these practices are not reported by minority nurses for fear of retribution. I was told once by a white manager that there are very smart and brilliant minority nurses but the fact of the matter is minority nurses are considered minorities and will be seen as minorities. What I took away from this statement was that if minority nurses were given a fair chance in the nursing profession, they would excel to great heights and their white counterparts become threatened. Let's call a spade a spade. My years in the nursing profession were riddled with racism and discrimination.

Many of the minority nurses I have worked with for twenty-two years have experienced the same injustice, humiliation, and mistreatment. They have been denied promotions and in some instances lost their jobs if they addressed the racism or discrimination they encountered on the job. My nurse manager was a great manipulator, a liar, and a bully; she was aggressive and uncompromising. It was her way or the highway. She made your life miserable if she was being challenged or you stood up to her. She was the devil from hell. If one should investigate the white VP's of nursing or nurse managers, you will discover they were horrible nurses who cannot think, solve problems, or lead effectively, but someone decided to place them in a job they are not qualified for.

Story #

20

The Lack of Diversity in New York City Hospitals

D. Rivera, RN, MSN, Bronx, New York

The population in New York City is one of a melting pot, yet the nursing profession in this city lacks diversity, and this is evident throughout many health care institutions. To meet the health care needs of such a diverse population, a culturally diverse nursing workforce is essential and crucial to the core of our nursing profession. For changes to be made within the twenty-first century, all minority nurses must assist in the fight to remove nursing practice barriers and tackle racism at its core. As a minority nurse, I give speeches to minority nurses, encouraging them to apply to facilities that promote multicultural working environments.

When I graduated nursing school, my concept of the nursing profession and working in the clinical setting was that nurses were hired based on their education, skills, and qualifications, not on their race, culture, or ethnicity. However, while we hope all people are included and considered for a job in New York City, we know this is not the case. Let's be realistic. The only fair game in life is death. It is a fact that we all die. There is no discrimination with death. It will come; the only differences are the cause, time, and circumstances. I have worked with minority nurses from all walks of life; the treatment is the same and considered the norm for many facilities. I remember working in New York City at a particular health care institution where all the managers were white. This facility had several floors where patients and nurses were all white, and minority nurses were forbidden to work in these segregated areas. It is very sad we are living in such a society where human beings are accepted based on the color of their skin, places of birth, and so on.

Minority nurses are only placed in all-white units, sometimes called VIP units, when a state visit is expected. This is done to portray some kind of diversity for a few days. Once the visit is over, it is back to business as usual. This is a shame and pitiful, but the hard reality is this is the lived experience of minority nurses in New York City. The grade for these institutions is F-. As I watched the Republican debate, I realized that suddenly everyone is concerned about mental illness in New York City as a motive of getting the people to vote. Many people in New York City do suffer from mental illnesses. The question is why? Have any of those politicians stopped to determine the possible causes? Have any of those politicians stopped to consider the fact that the widespread racism and discrimination in the city also contributes to mental illnesses. We can all treat the symptoms and the disease, but until we treat the root causes, no amount of money will cure mental illness. This is true and real within the minority communities, as well as the nursing profession. If we treat the symptoms and not the disease we are wasting resources.

How Racism and Discrimination Violate the Principles of the Nursing Profession

M. Latz, BSN, RN, Queens Village, New York

Working in New York City health care facilities as a minority nurse for eighteen years, I have experienced racism and discrimination that has been disturbing and violates all the principles upheld by the nursing profession. Years of mistreatment and injustice toward minority nurses on the job have fueled hostility and anger, not to mention the unequal access in career advancement and professional development. This ongoing practice in health care facilities, in many cases, is considered the norm by several minority nurses. As a result of the obstacles, mistreatment, and lack of equal promotion, minority nurses feel oppressed. Seeing how institutional racism has divided nurses in their profession is unsettling. Minority nurses have suffered from the acts of institutions and again from those of their white counterparts.

As I was writing my story to present to the author of this book, across my television screen came a story of an African American patient who was prematurely discharged from a hospital after repeatedly informing the hospital that she did not feel well and did not think she was ready to be discharged. The hospital moved ahead and discharged the patient anyway, and the patient immediately collapsed and died in the hospital's parking lot. The family is now looking into suing the hospital. This is exactly the same treatment minority nurses experienced on the job, except they do not die on the job. Of course, there may be unreported cases of deaths of minority nurses on the job from daily harassment. To go a step further, the death of the patient in the parking lot does verify how minority patients are treated within health care institutions in New York City.

I have personally seen minority patients moved to other units who have not fully recovered from their admission illnesses, just to make beds available for white patients. Minority nurses and minority patients have greatly suffered in these racially inclined institutions, and this needs to come to a halt. It is my hope that all minority nurses will continue to highlight and promote awareness of their experiences of racism and discrimination in the workplace at all times.

Removing Obstacles in Nursing Practice

S. Thompson, BSN, RN, New York City

The nursing profession in New York City in which minority nurses work is one of disgrace and horror. I am truly ashamed to mention to people that I worked in New York City hospitals because of the increased racism that exists and the maltreatment of minority nurses on the job. The questions I have for those who are experiencing these problems right now or in the past are: Did you observe the mistreatment of minority nurses on your tour of duty? Have you experienced personal and professional barriers? Have you ever been passed up for promotion, especially knowing you meet all requirements for the job? If your answer to any of these questions is yes, then welcome aboard; you are not alone. I have personally experienced all the above, working as an African American nurse in New York City. I have been in working atmospheres where morale is so low that patient care and outcomes are very poor as a result. The staff is not motivated to work or provide quality care; of course, we all know that with a motivated workforce, the results would be highly satisfied patients, positive outcomes, and good institution reviews. Institutions that foster motivation and value employees have better patient outcomes and happy, motivated workers.

The impact of racism and discrimination is so pervasive and pronounced in many of New York City's health care institutions that it can be easily identified by the layperson. Let's not forget that the first African American president of the United States, who holds the highest position in the United States, has fought tooth and nail to get his job done because of being an African American. Getting approval from Congress to perform his job was a struggle, yet he was able to remove obstacles along the way to get his job done. Each time this president attempted to do something that would benefit all the people, he was met with trials, obstacles, and name-calling, but he rose above them all. We as minority nurses need to do the same thing. We have fought the battle and run the race; now we have our crowns, so let's wear them.

Story #
23

Using Faith to Overcome Racism on the Job

O. Rojas, NP, Staten Island, New York

Working as a minority nurse in New York City has been a challenge, but my strength in my faith has helped me to succeed in my career. I have enjoyed my job despite all the odds. As a retired minority nurse, I am sharing my story with many of you who are still going through this ordeal. I know without a doubt that racism and discrimination have been widely practiced and reported to the various authorities who could do something to rectify the situation. Some have attempted, and some have done nothing. I, like many minority nurses, have made several complaints to the Equal Employment Opportunity Commission (EEOC), and these complaints were just swept under the rug. *Racial silence*, as it is sometimes referred to by minority nurses, is being covered up and in many instances not reported because of the fear of retaliation or victimization. What many health care institutions have failed to realize is that ultimately it is costly to them, because lots of money is spent on orienting new nurses who later resign after a month or two, increased sick calls by nurses, and poor patient-care services. Both parties will suffer, but a health care institution will have a higher financial loss. Therefore, it behooves institutions carrying out these practices to take a stand and implement diversity in the workplace with equality for all.

With an increase in lawsuits, some institutions are making strides to correct decades of these practices that have destroyed health care and the nursing profession. Eliminating racism and embracing diversity, along with promoting equal opportunities, will enhance our health care services and strengthen the nursing profession. Working to overshadow nurses' dreams and aspirations to do the best job they can do, as well as any form of racism or discrimination, violates nurses' rights to practice freely and as a result constitutes a failure of our health care system and patient care outcomes. Take control of your professional lives and those who attempt to stop you, show them you are unstoppable. Keep rising to great heights.

Story #

24

Failure of Local, State, and EEOC Officials to Fight Discrimination on the Job

J. Fernandez, MSN, RN, Brooklyn, New York

I am a Filipino American who has experienced severe racism and discrimination on the job throughout several health care institutions in New York City. Despite laws in place designed to inhibit this practice, complaints are not being addressed or investigated by our state and local representatives. I personally have and know other colleagues who have made several complaints to the Equal Employment Opportunity Commission (EEOC), and either these complaints were not investigated or the institution has some friend within the EEOC who totally disregards our complaints. I have discovered making complaints to the EEOC is not only a waste of time but a waste of taxpayers' dollars. This department does nothing to help those who are in need of their services. I have seen Hispanic, Caribbean, African American, Latino, Russian, Chinese, and various other minority nurses who have run into problems make complaints to several authorities, including the EEOC, and their efforts all went nowhere.

At the EEOC office, all the representatives were white; therefore the expectation of receiving help as a minority nurse would be zero. Because the EEOC was comprised of all whites, at least in my area, Long Island, I truly expected no assistance to my complaints, and that was what I received—no help, not even an investigation. Minority nurses are much better off working for themselves by opening their own businesses or seeking diversified health care institutions in which to give their services.

The other option for minority nurses is to work in unionized hospitals where they will have union representatives, even though some institutions work hand in hand with some unions. Some union delegates work at the same institution and therefore need to protect their jobs. This makes fighting cases of racism or discrimination within such institutions difficult and challenging. What has become of affirmative action and diversity in New York City? They all have failed minority nurses who day in and day out are striving to provide care and keeping people alive. At a unionized hospital a little help is better than no help in fighting racism, discrimination, and situations where you may be fighting to keep your job.

Story #

25

A Minority Nurse's Experience of Racism and Discrimination in the Workplace

L. Watson, RN, BSN, New York City

Racism and discrimination—I have seen them, experienced them, and lived them in the supposedly greatest city in the world, New York City. I was born in Guyana and migrated to the United States when I was ten years old. I attended school in New York City and have experienced racism from elementary school all the way to nursing school. I rose as far as director of nursing in one of New York City's hospitals, and it was then I experienced true racism. As the director of several units, I was told to hire white nurses on the day shift and minority nurses on the night shift. As an educated nurse, I did not condone this practice. After my white managerial peers realized I was not doing what I'd been instructed to do, I started to receive resistance on the job and threats of losing my job or being demoted. I firmly believe in developing a culture that promotes staff morale and creates future transformational leaders on the job. The threat of possibly losing my job did not faze me, because I knew as long as I was a nurse, I could get a job anywhere in the world. I stood my ground, refusing to carry out such an order. After another four years on the job, I moved to another

New York City hospital that did the same thing and subjected minority nurses to different terms and working conditions, doing the ultimate harm by segregation. Anyone who complains about the treatment of minority nurses will either be retaliated against or demoted; in some cases, they lose their jobs.

For many minority nurses, complaining is not an option because they have seen the aftermath of complaining or questioning the unlawful practices that riddle the nursing profession in New York City. Giving up the fight simply empowers those harboring these practices to continue doing the same thing over and over again. My story ended when one of the wicked nurse managers I had in the past was my patient. Embarrassment and shame took over, and she confessed to her crimes and apologized on her deathbed, an apology I did not accept. Put them in God's hand. They will either confess to their crimes or suffer slowly. God is always my commander and chief, with him all things are possible.

How Qualified Minority Nurses Are Constantly Passed Over for Promotion

G. Thomas, MSN, RN, Queens, New York

Working as a minority nurse in New York City is tough, barbaric, and humiliating. There is no respect, support, or promotion of minority nurses, who in many cases, are highly qualified for promotion. Though I was one of the fortunate minority nurses who was capable and able to address racism and discrimination in the workplace, some nurses were not that fortunate. I had a family member who worked with one of the local state senators. I made that clear on all nursing positions I held in New York City, and this was my secret weapon against discrimination. I was living in Staten Island, New York, but the racism there was extremely obvious and widely practiced so I decided to work in a hospital in New York City. Even though minority nurses were mistreated and racism existed, I took offense to situations where patients started calling nurses names and requested to have white nurses care for them instead of minority nurses. I do not put all the blame on the patients because this was what they had observed in the workplace and what was being portrayed in terms of the lack of diversity in the workforce. White managers jumped to the idea of replacing minority nurses with white nurses at patients' requests.

As a matter of fact, this is encouraged in the workplace and managers will then inform you, "I will change your assignment because you had a problem with the patient." Instead of managers intervening and explaining to patients that we are also qualified, skilled nurses, the resolution was to change our assignment and consider the minority nurses as a threat of some sort or a problem to patients. The bottom line is that if health care institutions keep promoting racism, segregation, and discrimination in the workplace, patients will in turn do the same thing at a different level.

Story #

27

No Equality in the Workplace for Minority Nurses

P. Donahue, MSN, RN, Brooklyn, New York

The health care reform act demands a system that offers the highest quality of care to all patients; therefore, registered nurses should practice to the full extent of their education, training, and scope of practice. For minority nurses, this reform is nonexistent. Nurses should be full partners with other health care professionals, but how is this possible when minority nurses are not allowed equality among their white peers? Nurses statewide should be leading change and advancing health, but for minority nurses, these goals are being hampered in the workplace. Minority nurses do not have to accept and work in racially inclined institutions but instead should do their homework and look for institutions that promote diversity. There is a wide range of areas of nursing where their service is truly needed. There are positions in public health nursing, travel nursing, home care, nursing schools, and even doctor's offices, and in some situations, these positions pay a lot more than hospital settings.

I was once told by a white nurse manager, "If you do not like it here, you can go back to where you come from." These managers need no reason for their smart comments but the fact you are a minority from a different country, your skin color is different, and you speak a different language. I have heard patients in the same institution, telling minority nurses, "Go back on the banana boat to where you came from." So you see, monkey see and monkey do. I have sought and worked at institutions where my service is appreciated and valued. I encourage other minority nurses to do the same.

Today I am a home-care nurse and love it. Not only am I able to choose the areas I want to work in, I have more autonomy that I did not have in hospital settings. Guidelines to enforce diversity and eradicate racism and discrimination is seriously needed in the workplace of minority nurses. The constant harassment, discrimination, and racism on the job has forced some minority nurses down the wrong path to drugs or alcohol consumption. The New York State Office of Professional Services developed a confidential program to help licensed professionals who are suffering from chemical dependency before they harm themselves or patients they provide care to. Have they investigated what may be the cause or what contributes to chemical dependency in the workplace?

For minority nurses, the ongoing racism and discrimination have led some down the path to narcotic, alcohol, and other chemical dependency as a way of dealing with the problem. Why then have they not developed guidelines for preventing racism and discrimination in the workplace? Instead, New York State is more focused on having professionals surrender their licenses. Why do we have an office of professional services when it appears this office is not effective in supporting professionals? After all, we taxpayers are paying their salaries for doing nothing. This is an agency that needs a complete overhaul.

A Call for Minority Nurses to Take on Managerial Roles

T. Topkins, MSN, RN, Staten Island, New York

Working in New York City, I was very lucky to be in an institution where I worked under a minority nurse manager. I have seen this nurse manager in action and loved her management style and the way in which she inspired all nurses—minority and nonminority. In the end, she took a good flogging for promoting minority nurses and ensuring that there was equality for all nurses. As a result of her managerial style, she had fewer sick calls. Her unit was such a great success that other managers became envious of her. Her secret weapon for her unit success was respect, building of relationships, and valuing her employees' input in decision-making processes.

For years, I observed her experiences on the job as a minority nurse manager who paddled her way in her role. What I have learned observing her has prepared me for any nursing role in any facility in New York City. This particular nurse manager was a true leader who inspired and motivated us to respect our peers. She encouraged us to pursue advanced education and improve our skills; moreover, she made us feel that we were a part of the team. Her Press Ganey score (a rating provided by patients for the services and care they receive at health care facilities) skyrocketed, and her unit exceeded all other units within the institution. Other managers were curious as to what she was doing, but truly all she had done was to diversify her staffing mix, communicate with her staff regularly, promote from within, value and promote based on qualification not friendship and make everyone feel valued and appreciated. By implementing these simple steps, she made her unit a success.

Within this institution, she was the only manager who promoted minority nurses. White nurse managers constantly overlooked minority nurses for promotion. Having such an effective manager who encouraged diversity and positive working environments will ultimately attract employees who want to be part of the team. The end result is increased employee morale and productivity, increased customer satisfaction, and a positive working environment. Her teachings have helped me in my nursing career, and today, as a nurse manager myself, these qualities stay with me. Therefore, I am pleading with other minority nurses to follow in our footsteps and help to make a difference in the workplace for minority nurses.

My overall observation when I was a new nurse was that white managers tended to belittle minority nurses and perceived them as not knowing anything. They tried to tolerate us, especially when they had no other nurses to get the job done, but we all knew their true motives. I encourage all minority nurses to go out there, be unstoppable, and do what it takes to honor your profession, values, and beliefs.

Story #

29

Turning Racism and Discrimination into Positive Ventures

C. Moniran, BSN, RN, Long Island, New York

I have decided to tell my story of my experience as a minority nurse in New York City in the hope that it will reach minority nurses who are going through the same or similar problems on the job. After graduating nursing school, I went on the job as a registered professional nurse and I was taught lessons not pertaining to nursing. These lessons were *racism* and *discrimination*. This was so blatant that patients and visitors could all observe it and at times would comment on their observations. I stood firm as a minority nurse to overcome and face these obstacles on a daily basis. I realized that as practicing nurses, our minds are just as important to nurture as our bodies.

When confronted with racism or discrimination on the job, I turn it into a positive learning experience to achieve positive outcomes. Ways you can do this include setting goals for yourself, advancing your education, and getting on a road map to complete or pursue an advanced degree. If you are an LPN, get a BSN; if you have a BSN, get an MSN and so forth. Keep improving your life and educating yourself so when the right job comes along, you will have choices in the kind of job you want. I had only been two months on my first job when I was hit in the face with racism. I stood up to my white manager, who was not only surprised I stood up to her but was fearful of her job because I had a bachelor's degree and my manager, who was white, had an associate degree. There was a sense of jealousy. She made the comment to me, "You will not get too far in this profession with your attitude." My attitude, in her mind, was that I stood up to her.

Today I own my own adult day care for elders and am the associate director of nursing at a magnet hospital. I have proven this nurse manager wrong. I wonder where she is today. I am proof that minority nurses are just as good, educated, competent, and skillful as their white counterparts and can do anything they put their minds to. I have used my position to inspire and motivate other minority nurses to grow professionally, enjoy their profession, and work hard to achieve their goals. Like anything else in life, you can win if you have a game plan. I have seen the results of how my work has helped to foster and promote strong, ambitious nurses who are now nursing directors, VPs of nursing faculties, and the list goes on. Do not stop and settle for less. Maximize your education and earning potential, and do not be fazed by what health care institutions do to dampen your spirit or momentum.

Story #
30

A Minority Nurse's Love for the Nursing Profession

S. Morgan, RN, BSN, Bronx, New York

I love being a nurse. I love what I do. I am kind, compassionate, and caring, and all the values I learned as a child were reinforced in nursing school. Moving beyond nursing school into the practice setting, I was stunned to see the racism and discrimination within the workplace against minority nurses. I was born in Tobago, so you know my skin color is dark chocolate. On the job, minority nurses' assignments were vastly different from those of white nurses. Our assignments were more of the chores of a kitchen maid instead of those of a registered nurse. Segregation was notably obvious.

White nurses were offered positions on the day shift, while minorities were given positions on the night shift. Many days, after my tour of duty, I asked myself, "Does this institution deserve my time and services?" I discussed my day's experiences with my family, telling them the truth of what was going on in this health care institution. My mother was not at all shocked when I explained the horror stories to her. She told me this was how it had been in the United States since she set foot here thirty years before and not to expect any changes, even in my profession. I refused to accept my mother's acceptance of this practice. I went back to work the next day with a vengeance, wanting to change this institution's practice.

These stories of minorities have become so common in the nursing profession. My plan was to meet most or all of the minority nurses working on the night shift. I decided to wait outside the hospital and explain to nurses what I was planning to do. I wanted to get their signatures and ask them to plan for a protest outside of the hospital. After three days, I had collected 123 minority nurses' signatures and provided a date of protest and no work. The institution in question was severely affected financially, and yes, patient care was compromised, but that was our only method of sending a message since it seemed no one else was going to be concerned otherwise. A month later, there was some diversity within the hospital and our work was appreciated and valued. Though this was a tedious ordeal, it did send a message to this institution.

Story #
31

Minority Nurses Continue to Fight for Equality and Justice in the Workplace

J. Fernandez, RN, MSN, New York City

Before I begin to tell my story of racism and discrimination against minority nurses in the workplace, I must first sincerely thank other minority nurses for telling their stories of the injustice bestowed upon them while working in hospitals throughout New York City. I have heard people mention that minority nurses should not work in hospitals in New York City because of the racism and discrimination; however, I strongly suggest we do work where our services are needed but fight the racism and discrimination that is common practice within these institutions. Thumbs up to those minority nurses who fought before our time for equality in the workplace and to those who are still carrying on the fight.

A warning to all minority nurses—all nurses make mistakes, yet as a minority nurse, making a mistake on the job means a resignation letter or firing for you. For the white nurses, it means a verbal warning and their jobs resumed. Be aware that you have rights, and when this happens, you can seek help from your union delegates or legal representation. The hospital I worked for is constantly hiring and firing nurses even for the least infractions. I have been a nurse for twenty-eight years. The only way to describe my experience on this journey is pure hell. I hated my job, and other minority nurses also hated their jobs at this particular institution. It had gotten to the point where I would say to people, "I would not recommend my worst enemy to be in this profession." I later realized it is not the profession but the institutions in which you work that harbor these practices and make the lives of professionals miserable.

We all need to take responsibility for our lives, and once we do that, everything else will fall into place. Do whatever you enjoy doing, and if nursing is it, make it work. Do not be pushed out of a job; leave on your own terms. Keep mastering your craft, and make appropriate choices to get to where you want to be in your profession. I have worked in several practice areas of nursing and enjoyed the skill sets I have acquired to perform my job with positive outcomes. All minority nurses need to take action on the job when racism or discrimination takes a hold on their nursing career.

Story #
32

Tough Road Ahead for Newly Graduated Minority Nursing Students

P. Tchorzews, RN, MSN, Queens, New York

I am a newly graduated minority nurse who was fired from my first nursing job after fourteen months. The reason given was that I was not moving fast enough on the job. However, I knew I was fired because I was an African American nurse who was working among a 90 percent white peer group on the day shift. I was offered a position on the night shift, which I refused, and it was shortly after that I began to experience problems on the job and was reprimanded for the new found reason of not moving fast enough on the job. It was difficult to see where I was going wrong because there was no prior feedback as to my job performance that led to my firing. As a newly practicing nurse, I have seen the discrimination that other minority nurses have experienced and watched them being fired quickly without substantial reasons.

On many occasions, I thought of taping conversations and comments with racial connotations made to minority nurses by white nurse managers and administrators. I knew this profession was not a glamorous one; however, my love for people and helping others was what inspired me to become a registered nurse. It was my zest for making people's lives better by improving their health, and doing so helps me to move beyond the torture and horrors of nursing. Although I have bad and good days, the positive outcomes and the satisfaction I feel from taking care of my patients outweighs everything else. As a nursing faculty member, I spent countless hours teaching minority nursing students how to weather the stormy road in nursing, stay true to themselves, and continue the trend to help those requiring their services. As a new grad you will be tested and tried but just as you conquer your lesson plans and exams in nursing school you can do the same on the job.

How Lawsuits Can Bring about Change in Racism

B. McMillan, MSN, RN, Brooklyn, New York

Kudos to all my minority nursing colleagues who have gone the mile to fight racism and discrimination on the job. I am an actively practicing nurse in New York City and have also experienced hard-core discrimination on the job. The first time I experienced discrimination on the job, I stood up and fought back. I will fight going down rather than sitting doing nothing. I went ahead and sued the institution that discriminated against me and won the lawsuit; the hospital settled out of court. This institution paid and paid well. It was a battle well fought and a message this institution will never forget. To all minority nurses, when you experience these problems on the job, be sure to keep dates, times of events, and the names of witnesses if any. I say this to let others know there is light at the end of the tunnel. Do not give up your fight. Persevere for justice and equality for minority nurses and for nurses who will follow after us. Support each other when segregation exists, work as a team, and watch each other's back. Look out for one another, and inspire and motivate each other. Be strong and encourage each other, and boost each other's morale when attempts are being made to trample on you.

Seek managerial positions so you can be in a good position to facilitate changes in the nursing profession for minority nurses who are widely underrepresented. I do have a mind-boggling question for the New York State Nurses Association (NYSNA), who developed a statewide peer assistance brochure for nurses. The question on this pamphlet asked: Do you know a nurse who is affected by alcohol- or drug-related problems? SPAM can help. SPAM is a resource for individual nurses affected by alcohol and drug-related problems or mental health problems. It is also a resource for schools and health care facilities. The one thing I agree with in reference to SPAM is every nurse deserves access to treatment programs. This is also true in the professional world of minority nurses in which there should be equality and justice for all. So NYSNA, how about a pamphlet that states: "Do you experience racism or discrimination, or are you passed over for promotion on the job? Then we can help." The same way problems of alcohol- and drug-addiction need attention, so do problems of racism and discrimination on the job. For all we know, the day in and day out of racism and discrimination on the job may well contribute to the use of alcohol and drugs. To all minority nurses, avoid this path of drugs and alcohol. Go spread your wings and explore as many areas of nursing as you can so you will be marketable for career advancement.

Story #

34

A Minority Nurse's Experience of Being Passed Over for Promotion

V. Singh, RN, NP, Staten Island, New York

I will delve right into my story and tell all as to my experiences working as a minority nurse in New York City. During my years of practice, the following were some of my experiences.

1. I was forced to work the late-night shift even though my white nurse managers knew I wanted to work days.
2. My schedule was manipulated so I could not attend school. My manager knew I was in school pursuing my master's degree.
3. Salaries for all minority nurses were the worst (meaning less than the white nurses'). I personally investigated the salaries of some white nurses, and some voluntarily discussed their salaries.
4. I was also discriminated against when I sought promotion and was told the positions were either already taken or they were interviewing candidates.

On this job, you will never be told when you are doing a good job, even when patients observe and comment on a good performance; rather, the managers will go looking for errors or mistakes, and this is when you become known to them. I find that the managers add more stress to an already stressful job. I would love to see the stories of more minority nurses from my institution in this book because there are so many stories to be told.

This institution I worked at lacks shared values and vision, diversity, a positive working environment, and motivated employees. There were several strong, experienced nurses who taught me how to keep persevering and not allow myself to be deterred from my goals and visions of my profession. We all formed a group and stayed focused and cognizant as to what was going on around us because there was always someone trying to segregate us or monitoring our every move to find ways to say minority nurses were not competent, a common defense used all the time to fight lawsuits of racism and discrimination. We remained the pillar of strength for each other and were unbreakable after seeing what went on in health care institutions in New York City.

Story #

35

Managerial Positions Given to Unqualified or Less Qualified White Nurses

S. White, RN, MSN, Staten Island, New York

Like so many others before me, I have experienced the poison of racism and discrimination that caused deterioration and destruction to the once-loved profession of nursing. I chose to tell my story because it has gotten to the point where young people do not want to go into the nursing profession because of the years of racism and discrimination in New York City. Lack of promotion for minority nurses was a major problem.

My nurse manager was a diploma graduate. I had a bachelor's degree, and my nurse manager was less qualified and had no leadership experience except that she was white. Within this institution, there were at least four other white managers with diplomas in nursing who were given management positions. The vice president of nursing (VP) had a BSN degree and there were other nurses within the institution with a master's degree. These positions are rarely posted, but instead given to less qualified friends and families of the hierarchy's managing the hospitals. They also should be held accountable and arrested for these underhanded tactics.

These managers were condescending, unsupportive, and racially motivated. They not only mistreated minority nurses but allowed racially motivated prejudices to influence their decisions and management style. Minority nurses were prevented from assuming certain roles within this institution and were allowed to work mostly on units with minority patients.

Many minority nurses struggled to get ahead in nursing because of the many barriers, the obstacles, and the red tape. Not so for me. I refused to wallow in this kind of practice. Heavy caseloads were given to minority nurses on the day shifts in hopes they would make mistakes and be fired or accept positions on the night shifts. In racially motivated institutions, you cannot let your guard down, because the one time you decide to let your guard down, they will definitely get you. For minority nurses out there, writing nurses' notes is essential.

During my practice, managers would go through minority nurses' notes to see if there were any deficiencies or anything they could catch them on. They were unable to find reasons to fire or humiliate minority nurses, and embarrassing us was very difficult because we assisted, supported, and guided each other. They hated this because the expectation was that they would find something to pin on us.

Overall, I think they were quite surprised that minority nurses were very good at writing their nurses' notes. I encourage minority nurses who are weak in this aspect of nursing to seek assistance before taking their first job. This is a skill you should and must master to survive in this profession. Finally, pray you get in an institution that values your skills and education, respects you, and promotes diversity in the workplace.

How Racism Contributes to My Dislike for the Nursing Profession

G. Perricon, MSN, RN, Long Island, New York

I am a late bloomer minority nurse who went into the nursing profession in my early forties, and honestly, I never enjoyed it. Nurses do eat their young—from nurse managers to staff nurses— and the truth is I stayed in this job to be sure I had health coverage and an income at retirement. I was known on my unit to be a "no-nonsense nurse" because unlike other minorities, I stood up to the racism and discriminatory practiced on the job. I was working in a critical care area of my hospital and complained about the lack of diversity, the racism and discrimination.

I wrote a letter to the president of the hospital, who indicated he was not aware of a racially discriminatory workplace for minority nurses. I find it hard to believe he was unaware; as the president of a hospital, he had to at some point have toured the facility to see what was going on. However, I think he eventually investigated, and a month later, the staffing mix was more diversified. All units throughout the hospital were reflective of minority nurses; the numbers were not equal, but the change was noticed throughout. Prior to this change, nursing assistants and receptionists were the only minorities on the units. After that, we did have minority nurses on these units.

As nursing education changed and nursing students were assigned to hospitals for clinical experiences, minority nurses became of some value because these students had to be assigned the bachelor-degree-holding nurses and many of the minority nurses met this criterion. They were suddenly appreciated. Several of us refused to be used in this manner and declined to precept the nurses; though this affected the students, the whole idea was to send a message to the institution that we would not be used in situations in which we did have some control.

37

The Destructive Effects of Racism on the Nursing Profession

O. Michels, RN, NP, Bronx, New York

I was inspired to tell my story when a friend of mine called me and informed me someone was in the process of writing a tell-all book about the experiences of minority nurses in the workplace. I contacted the writer and told her of my interest in adding five of my stories and that I knew other colleagues who would love to add stories. She replied, "I am about to stop taking stories," but I convinced her she would love my story, and she agreed to add one of my stories to her book.

The next day, I decided to write my story. It was the same night President Obama gave his 2016 State of the Union speech. I thought it was fitting for me to incorporate it into my story. I took the day off to watch the speech but fell asleep prior to watching it. My twenty-year-old son, who was at home, woke me and said, "Wake up. The president is on." He said, "Look at the audience with all those hatemongers; it is written all over their faces!" My son's observation was right on the money.

I turned to him and said, "Pay no attention to them. Look at the minority president who has risen to the top. As much as they may hate him, no one can go up there and be so poised." His tone, style, and speech was like no other. Those of the audience who were angry, it was just jealousy and fear of what he had done and could do given exclusive opportunity to do his job. Of course they did not expect him to serve a second term, but he proved them wrong.

As I continued watching the speech, I noticed Paul Ryan, who is paid with our tax dollars and is responsible for bringing the country together, with racism notably written all over his face; his demeanor and attitude are ones this country should not embrace and are a disgrace to America. He has this cunning grin on his face as if he does not want to be there. Then why attend? The president is only tolerated by many in the audience because they have no other choice. This is exactly how it works in the nursing profession for minority nurses; we are tolerated when there is no other option.

Just as the president's hands were tied by Congress, preventing him from performing his job effectively throughout his presidency, minority nurses in the workplace are prevented from doing their jobs. Everything the president touched on during his speech was absolutely correct; however, I was expecting him to really elaborate more on racism in this country. Until this problem is placed at the forefront as a major issue in the United States, the many issues of equal pay, equality, jobs, and health care for all will not come to fruition. This is the story of an Asian American as it also relates to the minority president's journey as the commander in chief.

Why New Nurses Don't Stay on the Job

L. Cormatinati, MSN, RN, New York City

Racism and discrimination are rampant in New York City, especially in the nursing profession. Health care institutions that encourage these practices are dangerous for America. I foresee the day when a nursing shortage will hamper the nursing profession and those who condone this practice will be on their knees begging minority nurses to work. This nursing shortage is just around the corner. Contributing factors include low wages and inexperienced younger nurses who leave the job after working only a few years. Racism and discrimination only promote violence, terrorism, and hatred. The minds of patients, families, and employees are poisoned with racism and discrimination. It is a constant battle on the job, fighting this plague called racism. Minority nurses are not allowed to excel for fear of our extraordinary capabilities.

Many of the nurse leaders I reported to know my capability and the capabilities of minority nurses in general. They knew if given a fair or equal playing field, we would not only rise to the occasion but also excel to great heights. I have risen to the height of my profession and was passed over on many occasions for positions I was qualified for while white nurses are placed in positions because of the color of their skin. I would be told the position was already taken. I looked at the minority attorney general, Ms. Loretta Lynch, who has risen to the top of her career. She is Harvard educated and met the qualifications for her new role but was kept on a string for days—the longest time ever in history for a chosen attorney general to assume her role—in part because she is a minority woman. This is exactly the same kind of treatment minority nurses experience on the job from white nurse managers. In the end, shame was marked on the faces of those responsible for delaying Loretta Lynch from assuming a position she was qualified for because Ms. Lynch stood her ground and outshone them all with grace, wit, tenacity, and intellect.

Racism is like the Ebola virus, which was attacked and stopped in its path. Though it is not completely controlled, tremendous changes have been made and major steps taken. Racism needs this same aggressive measure in New York City. Leaders in New York City lack credibility and have failed in their jobs miserably, not doing much to take on this fight. New York City ultimately suffers because racism diminishes the city in the eyes of many. The New York City system is rigged in favor of the whites; if you are a minority, it is just a constant battle to fight. We all must let our voices be heard and continue to fight for changes. We need to pay attention to make changes happen. We need to pay attention to how we all vote and for whom we vote if we are to see some effort in this direction of ending racism and discrimination. Let's all be undaunted by challenges and obstacles and make New York City the greatest city in the world where I can live as a Latino American.

Story #

39

Experiences of Other Minority Nurses

K. Dileo, MSN, RN, Brooklyn, New York

When I was called upon to tell my story and to discuss my experiences working in New York City as a minority nurse, I not only decided to tell my story, but I went ahead and contacted other minority nurses I have worked with in the past who have similar or worse stories. Because I was only allowed to provide one story to the writer, I decided to incorporate some experiences of other minority nurses I have worked with. I am from South Carolina but worked in New York City and have experienced vast amounts of mistreatment, prejudice, and discrimination at several institutions I have worked at in New York City and Manhattan.

These incidents of racism and discrimination stem from hospitals from Lower Manhattan, Middle Manhattan, and Upper Manhattan in New York City. These hospitals are schools for racism and discrimination. We were assigned to perform housekeeping duties; we were even asked to mop floors. We would only get assignments to care for minority patients. In some instances, we were offered positions on the night shift versus the day shift and given schedules where we worked three twelve-hour shifts back to back—all this so we would make mistakes and then could be fired.

These institutions will use minority nurses to do travel assignments for six weeks or thirteen weeks, enough time to give newly graduated white nurses' sufficient time to complete orientation and be placed in full-time positions. With travel assignments, these full-time slots are on reserve for the completion of white nurses' orientation. This treatment goes a step further in that, if a traveling nurse contract is not yet completed and the orientation of the white nurse is completed, the managers will find some problem or blame to put on the traveling nurse, in most cases minorities, to get rid of them sooner. Minority nurses need to refuse to work for these institutions that foster hatred and racism and inflict such abuse and inhumane treatment on minority nurses.

Story #

40

Finding My True Passion within the Nursing Profession

S. Jacoby, FNP, Queens, New York

I worked in a step-down unit in New York City for eight years and went back to school to become a nurse practitioner (NP). To be honest, I would not be in nursing today if I had not changed my path in the nursing profession. As an NP, I get to make many decisions for my patients and have more autonomy in the care I provide for my patients as well as my professional growth and development. It is such a coincidence I am writing my story at this very moment as breaking news just flashed across my television screen describing how an African American patient died because of a shortage of nurses. I know—everyone knows—this is not the case. The real truth is that institutions put patients' lives at risk by not hiring nurses, especially if the candidates are not their choice of nurses—in this case, minority nurses. This particular institution I knew very well because I worked there for two years and was gone after those two years because of the increased hatred, racism, and discrimination I experienced, not to mention the plight of other minority nurses there.

I clearly remember a situation in which we were so short staffed that a patient suffered a massive heart attack and was found dead in his bed because the staff was unable to get to him in time. The family sued and won. The lawsuit was based on the shortage of nursing staff and the hospital's neglect of patient care and safety. In situations like this, you not only want to remove yourself from these jobs but also not be part of corrupt practices. Nor do you want to watch patients dying unnecessarily. Nurses work hard and see a lot of patients suffering, and this gets to them. They are left with no alternative except to remove themselves from the problem. Today I continue to practice as an NP and completely enjoy my job in a multicultural facility.

Story #

41

Lack of Respect for Minority Nurses and Patients

L. Hagman, BSN, RN, Staten Island, New York

Working in New York City hospitals for fourteen years, I have seen it all. Young nurses come and go. Many live with their parents so when they observe what's going on in these institutions, they tell themselves they do not have to put up with the racism, discrimination, and mistreatment and they take a detour. What kept me going as an African American nurse was the fact that I enjoy what I do. I also realized that many minority patients do not have the medical education to know what's best for them in terms of the treatment they received. I felt I had to be there for them. I have seen white doctors go into minority patients' rooms, demanding they do certain tests.

Many times, patients would verbalize their concerns, not understanding why some doctors were just barging into their room unannounced. I remember complaining to my white nurse manager, who just brushed me off as if this was not a big deal. Managers were insensitive to minority nurses and did not care much as to how they were treated. I have observed the lack of concern for minority patients and minority nurses and prayed daily that the madness within these health care institutions would stop. Have you ever worked at an institution and thought that if you should get sick, you would not want to be at that institution? Well, this is true of all minority nurses who worked at the institution in question. So many times we were so understaffed, especially when minority nurses were on duty. The nursing supervisors would have to call for overtime approval, and the VP of nursing who was white would say no to the only minority nursing supervisor, who we observed made several attempts to help us.

In addition, she would get her tail burned for trying to assist nurses. She was also more qualified (having a PhD) than all other supervisors on duty, including the VP of nursing who had a master's degree. Therefore, she was qualified to make much more than staffing decisions. Yet this was how politics worked in these institutions where jobs were given based on the color of your skin, your culture, or your nationality. There were other supervisors who were white and were caught up in the same pattern of mistreating minority nurses.

The VP of nursing, who tried to cut here and there to save money on the backs of hardworking minorities, took home a handsome bonus at the end of the year. I will pose this question to all white nurse managers. How do you sleep at night when you treat human beings like yourself this way? If you are able to sleep at night, I guarantee you that on your deathbed you may confess or, worse yet, suffer for the things you have done in the past. I have seen it happen where on one nurse manager's deathbed her confession took over. The VP of nursing was so envious of not having a PhD and went back to school and was struggling. Please be aware, all you minority nurses out there, a nurse manager or VP of nursing less qualified than you are should not interview you for a job in New York City. Instead they should provide someone with the same qualification to carry out that interview. The New York State board of nursing needs to update and provide all institutions with this information.

A Minority Nurse Discusses Her Discouragement with the Nursing Profession

P. Devon, BSN, RN, Bronx, New York

Trying to preserve the nursing profession is extremely difficult. It's a profession that many turn up their noses at in disgust. Rightfully so, it has gotten to the stage where I myself have started to do the same thing. The discouragement comes from the discrimination myself and other minority nurses endure on the job. We are constantly being overworked and given unrealistic work assignments in an effort to allow us to make mistakes. One year out of nursing school, I observed a patient die in a vest restraint, which caught the patient by the neck and strangled him. We were told by white nurse managers not to discuss the incident; the only difference here was that this patient was white and we were not the ones taking care of him. It was a white nurse caring for the patient. Had it been a minority nurse caring for this patient, that nurse would have been fired on the spot without question. I stared in anger as the minority nursing assistant wrapped the patient's body in preparation for the morgue. Aside from the lack of care the patient received, there was a shortage of nurses on that unit.

Some minority nurses felt it was more beneficial to the hospital to carry out their acts of racism and discrimination instead of staffing the unit with qualified nurses. Minority nurses have found a way out of this low-morale working atmosphere. Many have opted to move back to their native countries where their education and skills are appreciated and valued in diverse health care institutions. In the end, the institutions suffer the consequences of their actions by having no nurses to care for patients. We were all tested and tried, working in New York City; however, my take on this is that without tests, there will be no testimony. I have stayed in touch with several nurses who walked away from the nursing profession here in New York City, and they are doing much better mentally and professionally. As I look back on my career, I am still positive that nursing is my calling, and despite all odds, I will not allow anyone or anything to get in the way of my dream of being a nurse and the best nurse I can be.

The expectation during my nursing career is that minorities are not capable of being nurses and we are not supposed to be practicing professional nurses. Such expectations have strengthened me to stay true to myself. I will stay in my chosen profession and will not be going anywhere soon.

Story #

43

Minority Nurses with Advanced Practicing Degrees Are on the Rise

J. Maritsa, RN, MSN, Brooklyn, New York

For the past decade, minority nurses in New York City have been severely abused and discriminated against in the workplace. Despite research telling of the plight of minority nurses in New York City, this trend still continues in the twenty-first century. The demand for advanced-practice nurses, nurse educators, and nursing faculty is rising, and minority nurses should explore other options in nursing to continue their professional journeys. The future of our health care system should focus on education, skills, and enhanced quality of care. The system must be capable of delivering effective care by qualified health care professionals and not focused on the culture of the nurses.

To achieve the best health care system in one of the greatest cities in the world, there must be an increased mix of highly educated, culturally prepared nurses. Nurses should take time to recognize each other's skills and knowledge in a diversified workforce, which would create and pave the way for a patient-centered system with positive outcomes. The shortage of nurses throughout New York City can become a thing of the past if minority nurses are treated fairly and given equal opportunities in the workplace. Because of the previously mentioned problems, many minorities have removed themselves from the health care setting either voluntarily or from the frustration of working in a highly intense, racially inclined working environment. Some solutions to this problem include recognizing the challenges that minority nurses experience, making complaints, and then finding out what if any support has been offered to minority nurses. We must develop strict institutional guidelines and policies to help eradicate racism and discrimination in the workplace.

Nurses are the foundation of health care institutions, and without a solid foundation, there will be a broken institution about to collapse. I must mention that several of the racist institutions have since collapsed, meaning they have closed, and many more will follow. Why? Because as much as health care institutions are needed, God Almighty works in mysterious ways. Minority nurses should be credited, given awards, and paid handsomely for the work they do on a daily basis, but instead, they are hit smack in the face with racism and discrimination on the job. We all have lot more work to do.

Story #

44

Planting Seeds of Racism
in Nursing Schools

D. Ramdinan, ADN, RN, Long Island, New York

I was interviewed and asked to write a story about my experiences working as a minority nurse in New York City. I just wanted to be clear that though I decided to write this story, there are many more I have experienced and the same is true of my minority colleagues I have worked with over the years. I must not fail to mention that many of the colleges in New York City and throughout the United States are also responsible for the growth of racism in New York City. Several of these colleges have made no progress in admitting minority students, though many are qualified for admission. College admissions are rigged to exclude minority students. There is a saying, "What you sow is what you will reap." Colleges start planting these seeds of racism and discrimination in classrooms, and it spills over into the workplace. If minority students do get admitted, they are underrepresented and college life suddenly comes to an end for many minorities.

In the nursing profession, many more minority nurses are at the bedside than their white peers only because the white nurses do not want to get their hands dirty and go into management.

Minority nurses are met with obstacles for promotion, and that is the reason many remain at the bedside. White managers are promoted with diplomas and associate degrees into managerial positions while minority nurses with the same degrees and even some with bachelors and master's degrees are at the bedside.

If minority nurses are promoted, their journey is a dark path unless there are other minority nurses within the same institution who can offer moral support. Nurses should be promoted based on their performance and education and not on who they are. I have frequently seen the disrespect, lack of appreciation, and obstacles for advancement for minority nurses, but because of my love for the profession, I stayed in it.

Story #

45

How Minority Nurses Fight to Remove Racism from the Workplace

A. Brooks, BSN, RN, Bronx, New York

My experience as a minority nurse in New York City is as follows. I was a practicing nurse for ten years and received my master's degree in nursing. While I was working in a New York City hospital, a nursing director who was white was about to retire so I decided to apply for the job and was denied the position. I later found out the position was given to a nurse with only an associate degree and five years of nursing experience. The obvious prejudice and racism was enough to let me know this was not the institution where I should pursue my nursing career. I took my case to the EEOC, who told me the hospital had the right to hire whomever they wanted to hire. Where is the justice in New York City? What is the job of the EEOC really, and why are we wasting taxpayers' dollars to maintain it? Where are our elected government officials? In the same case the EEOC said I did not have any merit for a case, I retained an attorney and sued the institution. We were able to settle out of court. Getting paid a sum of money was not what I wanted.

I wanted to expose the institution for what it truly was; instead, the attorney went ahead and settled without my consent just to be sure he was paid for handling the case. I am reaching out to all minority nurses to follow their gut feeling when they encounter injustice, racism, and discrimination in the workplace. Turning our heads as if these problems don't exist only leaves more room for the growth of racism on the job. Racism in one city, town, or state means there is racism and discrimination everywhere, and this becomes the problem of everyone. Let's join together as one to fight this cancer that eats away at the nursing profession. I enjoy nursing. I am proud to be a nurse. It is the greatest, most-fulfilling job there is, and I refuse to allow ignorance, hatemongers and racism-inclined minds to get in the way of my professional growth and development. Follow your passion, path, and goals and you will succeed.

Shared Experiences of Some Minority Nurses

V. Brathwaite, RN, MSN, Queens, New York

In telling my story as a minority nurse working in New York City, I am also telling my story on behalf of all minority nurses who have worked and retired and those minorities contemplating entering the nursing profession. We cannot afford to let Dr. Martin Luther King Jr.'s dream fade away by giving up the fight. We must never stop fighting for equality and justice and find ways of removing racism and discrimination, which have saturated the workplace for nurses. Let's all join forces to fight for the same cause so that those who come after us will not experience this inhumane way of life.

My years of working in New York City as a registered professional nurse and the racism and discrimination I experienced have strengthened me and given me the opportunity to advocate for minority nurses and my nursing career. We all must be a catalyst for positive change in the nursing profession. Racism has ravished New York City and the United States in general. I sat among a few friends and watched the Oscars. It is fair to say racism has reached its peak. Am I to believe, or is anyone for that matter to truly believe, there are no minority actors or actresses out there who are worthy of an award? It only makes it true because the so-called judges are all white.

To fix this problem, we must hit where it hurts, the financial infrastructure of New York City, by boycotting and not spending our money there, especially in places that do not appreciate or value us. One motto we must never forget is the fact we are great, ambitious, educated, and talented. We need to start investing in ourselves. We need to start our own businesses, work for ourselves, and provide work for other minorities. Many days, as I look at the news, I see that racism exists even at the highest level in America with President Barack Obama. Yet even many who did not vote for him find ways to use him. We all know this is because of his influence and power.

We must all realize we have reached a point in our lives, professionally and financially, and have achieved the highest level of education where we no longer have to beg to get to where we should be. An Oscar, which is just a statue, is not needed to validate the work of minorities. Our validation and capabilities are very obvious and are seen by millions of people.

Story #
47

Institutional Racism and Injustice against Minority Nurses

Mills, RN, BSN, Long Island, New York

I worked in New York City as one of many minority nurses who experienced racism and discrimination on the job. What I have experienced is the brutality and injustice against all minority nurses in the institution where I worked. Injustice was more pronounced than racism, and real injustice is being played out when nurses experience discrimination on the job and complain about their experiences. One such case was of a newly graduated nurse with less than one year on the job, who, after experiencing discrimination on the job, went and filed a complaint with the EEOC only to have the case turned against her.

Despite her telling the EEOC what was going on in this particular hospital, no one visited the hospital in question; rather, they conducted their own investigation from behind a desk and were unable to get the necessary information pertaining to the nurse's case. It was much easier to place the nurse at fault. This poor nurse, after being victimized by the hospital over and over again, was eventually terminated. I knew for a fact this nurse was telling the truth because I worked at the same hospital for four years and everything this nurse described was absolutely true. This minority nurse was out of a job and had no money but still went to seek legal assistance. She was duped by an ineffective attorney who was working with the hospital. This is typical. When minority nurses make complaints, there are consequences and some form of retaliation.

Approximately one year later, the Office of Professional Discipline, Prosecution Division, of the State Office of New York in Long Island sent a letter to the nurse, stating she had somehow violated the HIPAA law and her license would be suspended. This nurse was railroaded by the hospital where she worked, the EEOC, the Office of Professional Discipline, and an attorney. As a new nurse out of nursing school, this would have been enough for her to decide to take an exit from this profession, but she persevered and found another job. She got another attorney and fought the suspension of her license and won. Bravo to this young, inexperienced nurse.

I have serious concerns regarding the handling of this nurse's case, especially by the Office of Professional Services, whom one would expect to assist this nurse in preserving her license. They did nothing to help but participated in railroading her over and over again. The New York State Office of Professional Discipline also stood by and did nothing except to easily suspend her license. This is also an office that is there to help professionals. Discrimination was noted at the highest level of the nursing profession in a case poorly handled. It's only fair to say with discrimination at this level we have a much more serious problem. An overhaul in the Office of Professional Discipline is needed.

Story #
48

Harsh Disciplinary Actions Taken against Minority Nurses Compared to White Nurses

G. Rosario, RN, ADN, Staten Island, New York

Minority nurses in New York City strive to protect themselves against legal trouble and provide all their patients with the best of care while staying focused on the standards of nursing practice; however, even doing this does not save the working professional nurse in New York City from problems and legal issues that many institutions bestow on minority nurses. This is part of their plan to frustrate minority nurses and eliminate them from the institutions in which they work. The disciplinary actions cast down on minority nurses are much harsher than those given to white nurses, leaving one to wonder if minority nurses have committed murder. In one such case, a patient complained that she had been slapped by a nurse and it was immediately assumed that I was the nurse who had slapped the patient. I begged my manager to take me to the patient so the patient could identify me as the nurse who did this, but she refused and suspended me until an investigation was conducted.

A week later, I was called back to work and an apology was offered. I immediately submitted my resignation and sought employment elsewhere. I was told by a colleague I was called back because the same patient had requested me by name, asking where the nice, kind nurse who had taken care of her a couple of days ago was. I was threatened by the hospital. They said that I had not given them adequate time when I chose to resign and I would not be paid. I turned to the person in the human resources office and said, "If I do not receive payment for my holidays and vacation, I will expose the hospital for the horror that goes on in this institution in terms of patient treatment, segregation of patients and staff, and much more." A few days later, I received a check by Federal Express.

I continued to expose this hospital and discouraged minority nurses from working at institutions that commit these crimes. Today, this hospital is now closed, a good decision, which has saved the lives of many. There are many more out there that truly need to be closed and someday it will happen.

Always Strive for Success and Be the Best You Can Be

M. Malacai, FNP

The ugliness of racism has put a dent in the nursing profession, and it is no different from a deadly disease called cancer that ravishes and devours the body, mind, and soul of those inflicted by it. I too have experienced racism, discrimination, and much more despicable treatment and injustice while working in several New York City hospitals. I have also been passed over for promotion, even though I have a master's degree. The position I applied for was given to a white nurse with less experience and a bachelor's degree.

The vice president of nursing (VP), who was white, was part of the devious plot not to promote me to a job I was highly qualified for. A few years later, the day of rejoicing came when the VP was escorted out of the hospital by security after a few years of gross incompetence on the job. Don't be mistaken; many of the white nurses, including the VP, are placed in these positions because they have pink-colored skin. The VP decided to accept a management position at the hospital where I am presently working. I was included as one of the managers on the panel to interview her; the tables had turned. At first, I did not recognize the name, but when she entered the interview room, you could see the shock on her face as our eyes locked and we both recognized each other. During the interview, she was practically begging for the job because she had been having difficulty getting a job for almost two years. The evil one does eventually comes around to bite one. I do not have hatred in my heart, because all that does is consume you like cancer. Instead, I feel sorry for those who embrace ignorance. I convinced everyone on the panel to give her the job. One, two, three months had passed before she finally decided to apologize to me. I responded, "No need. You did me a favor. Look at where I am now."

I shared this experience to let all minority nurses know that when opportunities pass you by, you must find your inner strength within yourself, because this frequently comes when life seems most challenging. Always remember only as high as you reach in life can you grow, and as much as you can dream, you will succeed. When you are confronted with obstacles, it gives you the drive to climb mountains. The road always seems long and impossible until you get to the end of it. Find the desire to win and succeed and the hunger to reach your full potential. These are your weapons to open any double-locked doors to professional development and success. Sticking together is a starting point to your progress, and working together is your journey to great success.

Story #

50

A Diversified Workforce Produces Great Success

M. Richards, MSN, RN, New York City

I am the final minority nurse to tell my story of the fifty nurses who decided to tell all about their experiences while working in New York City. Like many others, I have experienced racism and discrimination, the lack of promotion, being targeted, and attempts made to frustrate me on the job. My story would not be a story if I had allowed small-minded people or weak managers to take away the values, integrity, and confidence instilled in me as a child.

My advice to all minority nurses is to seek institutions that promote diversity, enhance the nursing profession, and provide the opportunity for minority nurses to transform themselves as scholar-practitioners in an effort to effect positive change in New York City and worldwide. As we spread our wings and fly like eagles, let's show the world who we are and what we are capable of as we burst with pride in our achievements. Keep growing personally and professionally. Continuing on the road of our professional journeys, let's strive to develop a collaborative approach to our profession.

We must make it our goal to apply ourselves in a positive, productive, and professional manner. As we all move forward with resolve and unwavering commitment to being the best we can be and to realizing and honing our full potential, let's hold our heads high and be proud of who we are. These words of wisdom and strength I leave with all of you.

Do not forget our almighty God who sees and hears all. Leave the troubles, challenges, and injustices you endure in his hands, and then sit back and watch him take control of the situation. There will be many more stories to tell when his work is done. Love and peace to all.

Conclusion

To all minority nurses, as I read your stories, I heard your cries, felt your pain and your disgust, and understood your anger toward those who caused you grief and helped to place obstacles and challenges in your path. We are all one, and united we stand. I say to all of you when confronted with ignorance or hate, greet your enemies with respect and be kind to them. Put your trust in God, for you will have a much happier, more fulfilled life.

Allow your values to guide you. Do not become cynical. Do not believe you are not valued and important. Believe in the power of change to move you beyond the next level. Work hard and play by the rules, and you will make it. We will all rise and fall together.

Although this is the end of your real-life stories, I do hope this book has created an awareness for other minority nurses. I hope it will strengthen, inspire, and motivate you to seek help and refuse to go down the path of drugs or alcohol. From reading your stories, it seems that this is the intended goal of those responsible for the racism and discrimination that overshadows this city. Stay strong, and be the best you can be. Remember to greet everyone with respect, peace, and justice for all. Stay safe, be well, and God bless.

—Melvina Semper, DNP

About the Author

Melvina Semper is a registered nurse who resides in New York City. She grew up surrounded by medical professionals, some of whom are nurses and doctors. Growing up, she wanted to be a nurse but was discouraged by friends and family who wanted her to venture out and study law instead. Oh, how she wishes she did! Not putting nursing on the back burner, she wishes she had done a dual degree in nursing and law. She is action oriented, and her need for excitement is unique, which tends to push her into new territories. When things gets tough, she gets going no matter how difficult the situation may be. She takes on challenges head-on with much success.

Melvina attended nursing school first for her bachelor's degree (BSN), then her master's (MSN) degree, graduating with honors, a knockout 4.0 GPA, and later her doctorate in clinical nursing practice (DNP). Overall, she had a good journey and exposure in the professional world of nursing. Most of her nursing experiences were in the areas of the intensive care unit (ICU), the coronary care unit (CCU), the medical intensive care unit (MICU), the surgical intensive care unit (SICU), the respiratory care unit (RCU), cardiac catheterization, and a bit of telemetry. After nine years at the bedside, she felt a need to move beyond that point. She did some nursing supervision and taught at various nursing schools. Melvina has taught more than six hundred nursing students at community colleges and universities. Her areas of teaching focus were critical care nursing, medical surgical nursing, leadership in nursing, fundamentals of nursing, community-health nursing, palliative and hospice-care nursing, and nursing NCLEX reviews. None of her past or present students provided stories for this book to avoid any conflict of interest.

She later realized nursing education is where her passion lies. It has become the most rewarding part of her entire nursing career and feels gratifying when on many occasions while visiting some health care institutions she is actually reporting to some of her students in leadership roles. However, Melvina says her greatest achievement was having her son and daughter, whom she is absolutely proud of and thankful for.

Printed in the United States
By Bookmasters